ADVENTIST CHRISTIAN SCHOOL
22751 BRAY RD
WILLITS 95490

# GREAT MOMENTS IN AMERICAN HISTORY

# From Slave to Cowboy

## The Nat Love Story

Holly Cefrey

ROSEN CENTRAL
PRIMARY SOURCE™

THE ROSEN PUBLISHING GROUP, INC., NEW YORK

Published in 2004 by The Rosen Publishing Group, Inc.
29 East 21st Street, New York, NY 10010

Editors: Jennifer Silate and Geeta Sobha
Book Design: Daniel Hosek
Photo researcher: Rebecca Anguin-Cohen

Cover (left), title page, pp. 6, 10, 22, 29, 32 Rare Book, Manuscript, and Special Collections Library, Duke University; cover (right) illustration © Debra Wainwright/The Rosen Publishing Group; p. 14 © Bettmann/Corbis; p. 18 Chicago Historical Society; p. 30 Library of Congress Prints and Photographs Division; p. 31 Denver Public Library, Western History Collection (X-21562)

First Edition

Library of Congress Cataloging-in-Publication Data

Cefrey, Holly.
   From slave to cowboy : the Nat Love story / Holly Cefrey.— 1st ed.
   p. cm. —(Great moments in American history)
   Summary: In 1897, while working as a train porter, Nat "Deadeye Dick"
Love tells a young boy and his aunt how he was born a slave, after
Emancipation became a cowboy renowned for his riding and shooting, and
wound up a Pullman porter.
   ISBN 0-8239-4375-5 (lib. bdg.)
   1. Love, Nat, 1854-1921—Juvenile literature. 2. African American
cowboys—West (U.S.)—Biography—Juvenile literature. 3. Cowboys—West
(U.S.)—Biography—Juvenile literature. 4. West
(U.S.)—Biography—Juvenile literature. [1. Love, Nat, 1854-1921. 2.
Cowboys. 3. West (U.S.) 4. African Americans—Biography.] I. Title. II.
Series.
   F594.L892C44 2004
   978'.02'092—dc21

                                                        2003005999

Manufactured in the United States of America

# CONTENTS

❦

Nat Love was born a slave in June 1854, in Davidson County, Tennessee. Nine years later, slaves in the United States were set free by the Emancipation Proclamation. Nat Love and his family rented land from their former owner. They were very poor. After his father died, Love left home to try to make a living. He went west to find work. Love was one of thousands of freed slaves who went to the land west of the Mississippi River to start their new lives.

Nat Love decided to become a cowboy. At that time, there were many African American cowboys. They did the same work as white cowboys. African American cowboys were also paid the same as white cowboys. Being a cowboy was one of the few ways for former slaves to earn the same amount of money as whites. Cowboys were very important in the West. They took cows from the ranches where they

were raised to markets where they were sold. Cowboys also had to break wild horses. Wild horses would jump and kick whenever someone tried to ride them. To break a wild horse, a cowboy would ride the horse until it got used to having a rider on it.

Love enjoyed riding horses and was ready for an adventure. He was an excellent rider and gun shooter, winning many contests. Love earned the nickname Deadwood Dick. People around the country heard about Deadwood Dick and his amazing feats.

In 1889, Nat Love ended his days as a cowboy. He became a porter for Pullman trains. His cowboy days were over, but not forgotten. Love was very proud of his skills and often told people stories about the many things he had done. Some stories were true, but some stretched the truth. All of these stories added to the legend of Nat Love as Deadwood Dick.

Nat Love worked as a cowboy for over twenty years. After he married in 1889, he quit being a cowboy and went to work for the Pullman Company.

Chapter One

# NAT AND NIGEL

Nat Love enjoyed working as a train porter. He liked traveling and meeting different people. On one trip in 1897, Love met an eleven-year-old boy named Nigel Brexal. Nigel was traveling with his parents, grandmother, and aunt.

One evening, Love entered the Brexals' car to clean up. He saw Nigel staring out of the window. As usual, Nigel's parents were in the dining car where they would stay for hours. Nigel flipped through a bag of dime-store novels.

"Which one is your favorite?" he asked as he walked over to Nigel.

"Without a doubt, it's *Deadwood Dick*!" exclaimed Nigel.

"Well, I'll be! Let me see that," said Love. Nigel handed him the book. Love looked closely at the

cover and said, "The real Deadwood Dick does not look anything like this man."

"My father says that most of these stories aren't true," Nigel said.

"I can't speak for other stories but...." Love lowered his voice and leaned in close to Nigel, "I can speak for Deadwood Dick because you're looking at him!" Nigel looked at Love in disbelief. "You don't believe me?" asked Love. "Well, look at this." Love lifted his pant leg to show a bullet wound. "I have fourteen of them all over my body," Love said.

Nigel's mouth dropped open. He had read about cowboys, but he had never met one before. Now he was talking to Deadwood Dick! Nigel's aunt, Barbara, was listening from her seat. "Please, sir, do go on. I love cowboy stories—whether they're real or not," she said with a smile.

Love nodded his head. "As you wish, Madam." Love pointed to a spot on his shoulder. "Another

bullet went clean through me here. It came from an Indian's gun," he said. Both Nigel's and Barbara's eyes grew wide with excitement.

"Indians!" Nigel shouted. "Did you have to fight a lot of them?"

Love laughed. "Yes, several times, but that's jumping ahead in the story. I think I should start at the beginning. If that's all right with you?"

"Oh, yes!" Nigel replied. "Is it all right, Aunt Barbara?"

"Of course. Please continue, sir," Barbara said.

"If I do tell you more, you'll have to call me Nat," Love said. "That's my name."

"Okay, Nat," Nigel said.

"I was born a slave in Davidson County, Tennessee," Love started. "Back then, no one would have guessed that a slave would be riding the range as a free man before his sixteenth birthday, but it's true. My story—the story of the *real* Deadwood Dick is all true!"

A Case of Breaking the Horse or Breaking My Neck

One of Love's jobs as a cowboy was breaking wild horses. That job earned him the nickname Red River Dick. This drawing is from the book that Nat Love wrote about his life, *The Life and Adventures of Nat Love.*

# Chapter Two

# CHAINS TO SPURS

"How did you go from a slave to a cowboy, Nat?" Nigel asked as he sat next to his Aunt Barbara.

"When I was about seven, the North and the South went to war," Love said.

"The Civil War!" Nigel exclaimed.

"Yes, that's the one. When the North won, we slaves were told that we were free. Slavery was outlawed. Father rented twenty acres from our former master. Life was really hard. All day long, I helped my father on the farm. At nights, he would teach us the alphabet."

"Were you able to go to school?" Nigel asked.

"Oh no. There weren't any schools for the black children where I lived. My father taught us all that

he knew. We tried to make the best of things. Even though we were so poor, we had each other and we were free. Things went from bad to worse, though. About a year after we were freed, Father got sick and died."

"You must have been terribly sad," Barbara said.

"Yes, but there was no time for tears. I became the man of the house. We had no money for clothes or seeds to plant crops. I had to get to work or my family would go hungry. I got a job for one dollar and fifty cents a month. It wasn't much, but it was all I could get then. I learned there weren't opportunities for blacks…and when there were, we would not get paid much for our hard work.

"It was about this time when I first started working with horses. I broke my first horse when I was about eleven or twelve. The Williams's ranch had several wild horses. There were two boys there about my age. They paid

me ten cents for every wild horse that I broke. I didn't know what I was doing. As soon as I was on the first horse, I knew to hold on for dear life—and I did. I broke a dozen horses for them!

"One day a man named Johnson held a raffle for a horse at fifty cents a ticket. I bought a ticket after selling two chickens. To my surprise, I won the raffle! Mr. Johnson knew I needed money more than a horse so he said he'd buy it back for fifty dollars. I agreed. He turned right around and raffled the horse again. I bought another ticket…and won again! He bought the horse from me again. I had nearly one hundred dollars. I gave my mother half. I told her I was going out into the world to make a better life. My uncle came to help run the farm. On February 10, 1869, at fourteen years old, I left home."

After the Emancipation Proclamation in 1862, many African Americans headed west in search of a new life. African American cowboys, such as Nat Love, were a common sight in the West.

# Chapter Three

# THE SADDLE BECAME MY HOME

"Gosh, you weren't much older than I am!" Nigel exclaimed.

"That's right," Love said. "I had to grow up quick after my father died. It wasn't easy to decide to leave, but I had to take a chance. I'd heard that freed slaves were finding luck in the West, so I headed there, too. I went to Dodge City."

Nigel looked at Love's hands. They were large, rough, and muscular. Nigel imagined that Love was riding on a horse, swinging a lasso. "Where is Dodge City?" he asked.

"Dodge City is in Kansas. It was one of the biggest cow towns of the time. Cowboys from Texas and all over the West ended up there at one point or another. That's where I became a cowboy," Love told him.

"How did you do that?" Nigel asked.

"One night, I watched a group of cowboys in a pub. There were some black cowboys in the group. I wanted to find out more about them, so I followed them back to their camp. The next day, I asked if I could join their group. The camp boss asked me if I knew how to break a wild horse.

"I said, 'Sure do, boss.'

"He laughed and said, 'We'll see about that.'

"Then, he yelled to one of the black cowboys, 'Bronco Jim, get Good Eye!'

"Good Eye was the wildest horse I had ever seen. I got on Good Eye's back and he gave me the toughest ride of my life. He bucked and kicked and ran in every direction. I stayed on him, though, and surprised every cowboy in camp. The camp boss offered me a job as a cowboy right away. He said he would pay me thirty dollars a month! That was more money than I had ever had. They gave me my first nickname, Red River Dick."

"But I thought your nickname was Deadwood Dick," Nigel said, holding up the dime-store novel.

"Well now, it isn't uncommon for a cowboy to be known by many names. My boss named me Red River Dick, but the people of Deadwood, South Dakota, named me Deadwood Dick. Just like breaking in that wild Good Eye, I had to earn the name Deadwood Dick," Love answered. "But that's later in the story. I'll get to that soon enough."

"Sorry, Nat," Nigel said. "What happened next?"

"After I was hired, the camp boss took me back into Dodge City and bought me a saddle for my horse, a blanket, and many other things I'd need. He even bought me my first gun. I was a real cowboy," Love said.

"Wow!" Nigel exclaimed. "I wish *I* were a cowboy."

"It's not all fun and games you know," said Love. "It's hard work and dangerous. I ran into danger my very first day on the trail!"

Deadwood, South Dakota, is where Nat Love earned his nickname Deadwood Dick. The town was named for dead trees found there. This photo shows the town in 1876.

*Chapter Four*

# DEADWOOD DICK

"What happened, Nat?" asked Nigel.

"After we left Dodge City, we headed to the ranch in Texas. We rode along the Sun City Lonesome Trail. A few miles out, it started to hail. The storm was one of the worst I have ever seen. Things got scarier, though, when through the hail, I heard the chilling war cry of Indians.

"Suddenly, we were surrounded by them! There were only fifteen of us and about one hundred Indians. I watched some of the cowboys fire their guns. They yelled at me to use my gun. Everything had happened so fast, I had forgotten to draw my gun. I quickly pulled it out and fired it for the first time. The fight felt like it lasted for hours. When it

was all over, we had lost all but six of our horses. We slowly made our way to the ranch. It was a long walk," Love said, shaking his head.

"Despite the rough start, I loved being a cowboy. There was always work to be done and an adventure to be had. When we weren't taking cows to market, we were moving them from one grazing area to another. On these cattle drives, we rode as much as eighty miles a day. We also practiced shooting whenever we had enough bullets.

"In the spring of 1876, we received an order to deliver three thousand steer to Deadwood."

"Three thousand steer!" Nigel exclaimed.

"Yep! We rode for two months through New Mexico, Colorado, Wyoming, and South Dakota. We delivered the steer to the new owners when we arrived in Deadwood. The next day was July fourth. The people of Deadwood held a roping contest since the town was filled with cowboys.

"The winner of the contest had to rope, saddle, and mount a wild horse in the shortest amount

of time. They chose the wildest beast for me, but I was riding him in exactly nine minutes. The next fastest time was more than twelve minutes. My time was a roping record, which has never been beaten, even to this day.

"That contest was so much fun that they decided to have a shooting contest. The winner had to hit a target with fourteen shots from a rifle and twelve shots from a Colt handgun. From more than a hundred yards away, I was able to hit the target with all fourteen rifle shots. I hit the target with ten shots from the Colt, but missed two. Even having missed, I won the shooting contest. I won two hundred dollars!" Love said.

"That's amazing!" exclaimed Barbara.

"I was named the winner, and people there gave me the nickname Deadwood Dick. As more people found out about the contest, my nickname spread. Soon, everyone was calling me Deadwood Dick," Love said with a smile.

In 1890, Nat Love (at far left) began to work as a Pullman porter, leaving his cowboy days behind. Pullman porters made sure train passengers were taken care of.

# Chapter Five

# Iron Roads Through the West

"I know you loved the work, but didn't the life of a cowboy make you lonely?" Barbara asked Love.

"Some days were lonelier than others, Madam," Love said. "However, I did almost get married twice. Once when I was captured by Indians."

"You were captured?" asked Nigel.

"Yes, I was. It happened a couple of months after I earned the name Deadwood Dick. A few of us were out on the range looking for stray cows. I was alone when I heard an Indian war cry. I saw a group of Indians heading for me. I rode as fast as my horse would take me, but they caught up. Bullets flew by me. One went through my leg and into my horse. My horse died right there. I fired

23

away at my attackers. I killed several of them, but I ran out of bullets.

"When I awoke, I was in their camp. They had put plants on my wounds to help them heal. The Indians kept me tied up at first. After several days, they let me walk around, but I was always guarded.

"I learned a lot about them. We mostly talked by using our hands. They told me that I was to marry the chief's daughter. She was a beautiful girl. They were going to give me one hundred horses for the marriage, too. It would not have been the worst thing to marry her, but I was a cowboy at heart. I looked for the first chance to escape. Finally, about thirty days after I was caught, I got my chance. I crawled to the pen where they kept their horses and I picked the best one. I rode all night, for about twelve hours, without a saddle, to my home ranch. I had escaped!"

"Wow, that's amazing!" Nigel cried out.

"The next time I almost got married was

when I was working near Mexico City. I saw a lovely Spanish girl standing in her yard. I fell in love with her immediately. I can speak Spanish just as well as I can speak English, so I introduced myself to her. She and I had a lovely talk. I met her several times. Soon, we were engaged. I planned to marry her and make a home for us in Mexico City. However, she got sick and died before we got married. My heart broke into pieces. I went back to my life as a cowboy, but I have never forgotten her."

"Oh, how sad," Barbara said with a tear in her eye.

"That wasn't the only sadness in my life at that time," Love said with a frown. "It was then that the iron road was laid."

"What's the iron road?" Nigel asked.

"The railroad, son," Love answered. "Because of the railroad, cowboys were not needed for long drives. Cows could be herded to the nearest railroad station and loaded onto cars. More settlers came out West. They claimed land that was once the open range. The ranches became much smaller and very few cowboys were needed. In 1889, I decided to look for a better life."

"It must have been hard," Barbara said.

"Yes, it was, ma'am. The buffalo were almost gone and the range was divided up among settlers. The land itself was a sad sight. I headed to Denver, Colorado. I met a wonderful woman named Alice there. We married on August 22, 1889.

"One year later, I got my job as a Pullman porter. I rented a small house for us. Alice sits there now, making the most beautiful quilts you've ever seen."

"How wonderful!" exclaimed Barbara.

"Yes, it is wonderful indeed," said Love. "I guess that's the end of my story. I hope it helped to entertain you."

"Thank you very much. You should write your own book, Nat," Nigel suggested.

"Yes, Nigel. Maybe I will," said Love as he turned to leave the car, rubbing his chin. "Maybe I will…"

# GLOSSARY

**acre (AY-kur)** a measurement of area equal to 43,560 square feet

**dime-store novel (DIME-stor NOV-uhl)** an inexpensive book

**Emancipation Proclamation (i-man-si-PAY-shuhn prah-kluh-MAY-shuhn)** an order signed by President Abraham Lincoln freeing slaves in the United States

**engaged (en-GAYJD)** having decided to get married

**lasso (LASS-oh)** a length of rope with a large loop at one end that can be thrown over an animal to catch it

**legend (LEJ-uhnd)** a story handed down from earlier times

**porter (POR-tur)** a person who waits on train passengers

**raffle (RAF-uhl)** a way of raising money by selling tickets and then giving prizes to people with winning tickets

**ranch (RANCH)** a large farm for cattle, sheep, or horses

**saddle (SAD-uhl)** a leather seat for a rider on the back of a horse

**steer (STEER)** a young male of the domestic cattle family raised especially for its beef

# Primary Sources

To understand the people, places, and events of the past, we can study different types of materials. For example, by analyzing old books, photographs, diaries, maps, and drawings, we can learn about history as it happens.

Sources such as Love's book, *The Life and Adventures of Nat Love*, can help us identify his point of view about life as an African American cowboy. By reading his book, we can also draw conclusions about the kind of person Love was.

Photographs are also important sources of historical information. For example, the photograph on page 22 identifies how Love dressed when he worked as a Pullman porter. It also shows us what train engines of the time looked like. Photographs are a very good way of helping us tell fact from fiction.

Studying sources such as old books and photographs help us answer important questions about events that happened years ago.

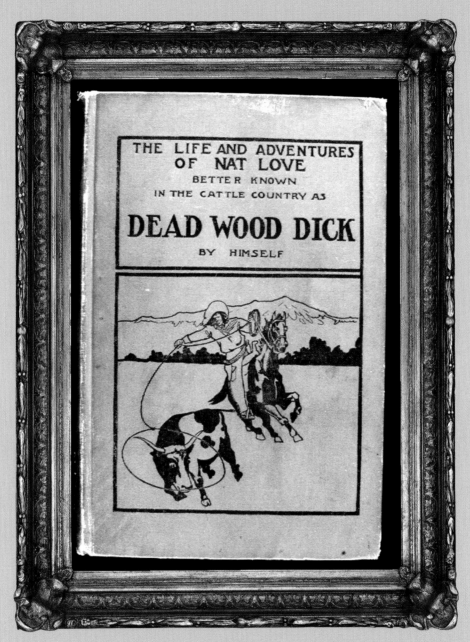

In his book (shown here), Nat Love tells of his many adventures and how he became Deadwood Dick.

This photo shows the inside of the first Pullman sleeping car, which was invented by George Pullman.

Once slavery ended, African Americans who moved west found many different types of work. Some, like Nat Love, worked as cowboys. Others, like these men, worked as U.S. deputy marshals.

My First Indian Fight

Life as a cowboy could be dangerous at times. Like other settlers in the West, Love fought with American Indians. The Indians were angry that the settlers were taking over their lands. This drawing is from Love's book.